THE NEW BIZARRO AUTHOR SERIES
PRESENTS

WINNIE

KATY MICHELLE QUINN

ERASERHEAD PRESS
PORTLAND, OREGON

ERASERHEAD PRESS
P.O. BOX 10065
PORTLAND, OR 97296

www.eraserheadpress.com
facebook/eraserheadpress

ISBN: 978-1-62105-254-8
Copyright © 2018 by Katy Michelle Quinn
Cover design copyright © 2018 Eraserhead Press

Printed in the USA.

Editor's Note

We all need comfort. Sometimes it comes as a cool beer, a warm bed, a cat curled up at your feet. Sometimes it comes as the raw destructive potential to drop any sucker that so much as looks at you funny. It is possible for our comfort to come at the expense of other people's comfort, peace or safety. It is possible to take comfort in sacrificing one's own comfort and joy for the comfort and joy of someone we love. The heroine of Katy Quinn's Winnie has devoted her life to providing comfort for the man she loves...by living as his rifle. What happens though when we evolve into something that is no longer comforting to those around us? Should we keep trying to maintain unconditional love or should we finally start to think about ourselves? Winnie must answer these questions and others that she hadn't thought of asking. Winnie is a story about love, our love for each other and our love for guns. Personally, I love this story.

—Garrett Cook, editor

THE ONLY GIRL

Colt tells me I am the only girl he'll ever want, the only one he'll need.

He takes me out to pasture, to fix a tear in the fence put there by cougars or dogs or fucking drunk teenagers again, driving past the lyrics of some awful pop country song fiddle-fast. That song plays on the radio of Colt's own old Ford, can in the cupholder, driving down dirt. But he's no teenager and he knows how to hold a Coors low enough the few cops around won't see it, and that makes all the difference.

He takes me into the forest to kill dinner. Pray for deer, but more often than not it's just a squirrel and sometimes nothing at all. I don't eat, but I always pray for deer. That way, when Colt holds me close, hands wrapping me tight, whispering *You got this girl, you got this Winnie, come on now just right through the skull and done,* and I aim, breathless, and let the round fly straight and true as God and America, Colt will be smiling when he drags it home. A deer falls flat, and he dances around and yips like a young imitation of the cowboy he is. He'll squeeze me to his chest and stroke me gently and say *good girl, I knew you could do it,* and everyone's happy and the well-fed sun sets kaleidoscopically over the quiet Rockies.

He'll lay me down on the ragged, spent bench seat of his Ford then climb into the cab himself and mutter it awake. The radio plays a Toby Keith song, and Colt sings to it in a voice that's a new nickel covered in mud. We drive into town, Ghost Town, the place he lives outside of, which is to say we drive to the gas station on the outskirts of it. Another carton of Marlboro, and a couple three eighteen racks of Coors to make it til Sunday. Ten minutes in and we're growling down the road back home, shuddering over bumps.

When we pull in home, Colt shuts off the truck and inhales one more whiff of its musk, finishes up his Coors for the ditch and tells me that I am the only girl he'll ever want, the only one he'll need.

I know this to be true. He tells me every night. After the fences have been fixed, dinner's been killed and cooked, and the drinks and darts have been slurped and smoked, he tells me this.

My favorite part of the day is the part where we sit silent on the porch of our little one-room cabin out in the nowhere of the inner Northwest, where mountains and trees blur the state lines and where you could hear a pin drop were there anyone out here to own one. Colt pats a belly packed with venison and taps the ash of his last cigarette of the night into his last Coors of the night. If I could speak I wouldn't, and he doesn't say much, either, but nights like this I know he's happy just watching the stars rise with me laying long across his lap.

When everything but the sky blacks and it gets too quiet for even a cowboy to handle, Colt lets out a loud belch and pushes himself out of his rocking chair and carries me inside like a young bride across the threshold. He pulls his handkerchief out of his Levi's pocket, spits on it, and begins to gently run it down the length of my slender, blue steel and walnut Model 1873 body. My wood turns to metal, and my metal turns to diamond. Colt starts to petrify as well, the zipper of his Levi's pulling taut. He pours some oil on the rag, begins to stroke me with quicker hands, a tighter squeeze. If I had eyes I'd close them. My walnut soaks up Colt's oils. His eyes don't tell me if he realizes what he's doing. He sits down on his bed and rests me between his legs, right next to his stiff denim member. He strokes me harder and I can feel the pressure building in my chamber, feel his hands oil me down once, twice more and then grasp me around the trigger and barrel like Johnny Cash around June's waist. He slides his rough fingers into the grip of my trigger and forces it down until I click. I could explode at any moment.

Colt puts my stock up to his shoulder and points me out of the open window of his cabin. The pressure in my chamber takes me over, a cowboy's weathered fingers injecting me with ecstasy.

Good girl, Winnie, Colt says and then he pulls my trigger and I expel everything inside out. A flash flies through the window, and the echoing of my gunshot whispers me and Colt and the night outside to silence.

When the echoes subside we let out our breath, long and slow. Colt takes a moment to look me up and down, then lays me down on the bed. He stands up, revealing that the stiffness in his Levi's has been replaced with a large, dark spot running down his right leg to almost the knee. He shimmies off his jeans, holds them up to examine the wetness, shrugs, and then hangs them on the back of a chair in front of the wood stove to dry. Standing over me like a backwoods Adonis in raggy Hanes briefs, Colt smiles, a thing cowboys don't do often, then lies down.

Night, Winnie, he says.

G'night, I say, knowing I'm in the only place I ever want to be.

GHOST TOWN

Ghost Town used to be called Evansville, and still was by anyone that had never been there. Sometime within the last twenty years or so, the agricultural economy that sustained its citizens passed out, and the generation that could've kissed it awake moved to bigger, more important places. The nickname Ghost Town was given in preparation for the inevitable. The buildings and their inhabitants had started to reflect the new name in their lives and appearances. Farmhouses that had been freshly painted a few summers back heard the name Ghost Town and began clawing off their newly painted skins, digging windhands into their own wood. Citizens that remained in town aged fifteen years in a day. The elderly went to sleep, knocked off, abandoned skeletons in their beds. Middle-aged men outgrew their crises and began planning for quiet retirement. Children unfolded their finger-guns and picked up rifles. All this because of the name that was given a thing. Ghost Town. Some say a name is just a word, but to others it's judgment and sentence, a town pronounced dead too soon.

COLT, AGE 12

It is a hot summer day on the farm of Buck and Gretchen Wilder. Buck is a third generation farmer and Evansville native. His father had worked this land with his bare hands, and his father's father had worked it before. It has always been hard work, but lately it is getting harder. The heat feels nice on the skin but means trouble for the crops. The grain is burning black, and the apples are dehydrating into elderly sacks of matte red skin. The cattle crouch in any shade they can find to avoid being prematurely cooked.

It doesn't make it any easier for Buck that his son is a burnout. Long time gone from here, and good riddance. A drunk with a poet's dream who fucked half of Evansville and by some mercy of the Creator only left one child abandoned on the farm of his parents.

Right now, Colt is only twelve years old and the blackening heads of wheat spark curiosity instead of the fear of agricultural bankruptcy. In the oversized shirt his father left him, ratty when he got it, worse now, he runs through the rows of plant corpses with his airplane arms out, whipping at what's already given up.

The world hasn't been taken from him yet.

It doesn't make sense to the young Colt why his grandfather yells profanities over dinner, smashing his fists into the bowls of gruel that should be meat, they deserve that much for all this work. It doesn't make sense why his grandmother only cries in response and doesn't yell back. It doesn't make sense why they keep setting an empty place for his father, a man who in his twelve years Colt has never once met.

The only thing that makes sense to a boy this young is that in the early dark of the night, when he has been put to bed, he has discovered how to hold himself in all the right places to make it all better. He can't even cum yet, doesn't know what that is, but he can build pressure inside himself like powder in a chamber with a quick flick of the wrist and the thought of his grandfather's gun rack, it contents shining silver when he opens its doors. It only takes minutes to achieve a meaningless release, and then he is tired, suddenly, and finds it much easier to fall asleep now, despite the screaming that can still be heard down the hallway.

He blinks himself to sleep because tomorrow is another day on an endless list of them, and around here, that's just what you do.

But tonight is not another night. Tonight will be known as the Aging for the next while, the night Evansville died. The Wilder's farm is not the only one on its last leg, in fact there are few that aren't, if any. The whispers of Ghost Town have spread through the citizens like a new kind of gospel. The question *are we dead yet,* the answer *yes.* By some force of magic or god, this proclamation turns true. The name begets the thing itself. Someone has called this place Ghost Town one time too many, and now it will show them just how dead it can be.

The young age, and the old die. Buildings collapse and sag, taking with them anyone inside. The Wilder's farmhouse is lucky, it does not fall, but its inhabitants are not so fortunate.

Buck and Gretchen Wilder, both well into their sixties, are sped to their end on wild horses. Their grandson will discover this when he wakes up a man of nearly thirty. He will marvel at the sinews his limbs have birthed, at the depth of his voice when he cries out, *Grandpa! Grandma!* as he pulls back the sheets to reveal two skeletons curled up fetally, facing away from each other on opposite sides of the mattress.

The sun will rise today, like it would any other, but it rises on the carcass of a town no one remembered in the first place.

Colt shakes off the rags of his torn open firetruck pajamas and puts on a pair of his grandpa's slacks and a shirt.

The porch creaks extra loudly when he steps outside to survey the damage done. Everything he sees is curled over in repose and grizzled grey. He sits down in the rocking chair his grandfather would frequent, and pulls out a pack of Marlboros still in the pocket of his shirt. He lights one and sucks in, like he's seen old Buck do, and exhales, attempting to make sense of the smoke.

GREG'S GR8 GUNS

With no grandparents, no purpose, and no memory of over half of his years, Colt found me.

My life begins the day Colt walks into Greg's Gr8 Guns, a store on the edge of Ghost Town. This is ten years ago now. As far as I can tell, I am nothing before Colt lays his eyes on me, pointing and asking Greg, a man who is suddenly a legal senior, *what about that one?*

Colt's blue cowboy eyes, those first words, give me first breath. The first realization of being *that one* and not anything other, a sense of self.

Greg looks behind him at where I hang on the wall, doing everything I can to flaunt the curve of my stock, the firmness of my barrel. Call me Raquel Welch dressed in blue steel and walnut. I see it working. As Greg squints at the sale tag below me, coping with fifteen years and a minus six prescription gained, I watch Colt's posture stiffen, his pupils dilating ever so slightly. He exhales a horny snort like a horse. He takes off the tan Stetson that belonged to his grandfather and holds it as inconspicuously as possible over the zipper of his Levi's.

Don't you want to hold me? I call from the wall. As if I don't know, but I want him to tell me. Use your words. Lay me on your lap, rag me down, and whisper exactly what you want me to do in your Johnny Cash rasp.

Greg chuffs then slaps himself in the forehead.

"Of course," he says. "She's on sale for five hundred."

Colt's eyes open wide. I can't tell if it is a wad of cash he is playing with in his pocket or his cock. Maybe both.

"Really? Well, shit. I'll take her."

The dark spots in the armpits of Colt's denim shirt grow. He tugs on his collar a bit.

That's right, cowboy. You try and play it cool.

Colt pulls a wad of hunnies from his jeans pocket and slaps them on the glass counter between him and old Greg. They make a damp squelch and are covered in a thick wetness. Greg, with his senior-discount hearing and sight, doesn't seem to notice.

"Alright, young man," he says, "she's yours! That's a Winchester Model 1873, so you better take care of her."

Greg picks me up off of the wall-hooks I am resting in and hands me gently to Colt. He takes me in his warm hands, still soft as a younger man's, and squeezes my barrel and stock as he does. His fingers float over my varnish, digging into the grain. I can't tell if I have never been held, or have never been held like this. In the heat of the moment, I discharge, unaware until now of the pressure that has been building inside me.

Greg drops behind the counter, then stands up again. He shakes his head and starts to chuckle.

"Good thing she wasn't loaded!" he says, wiping his

forehead dry. "Shit, son! But you'll learn to handle a rifle yet."

Colt loosens his grip on me, his face reddening.

"I'm sorry," he says. "It's my first time."

Greg laughs and punches Colt on the shoulder, winking.

"It's okay, son. At least no one got hurt. My first time wasn't so fortunate."

Colt smiles, looking at me up and down from every angle. I soak in every drop of his river-blue gaze. This appetite for me, it's new. The lusty eyes, the gentle hands feeling every latch and crevice. A foreign language I want desperately to learn.

Colt says thank you to Greg one more time before leaving the store.

As we walk out of the door, he pulls me close to him and whispers to me.

I'm going to call you Winnie.

I relax the slight heft of my figure into his arms.

Cowboy, I say, *you can call me whatever you want.*

WINNIE'S DREAM

It is a warm night, either summer or very close to it, and the sunlight through the windows of our little cabin is beginning to burn out, becoming a paintmix the color rainbow sherbet must taste. The air that had been thick with caws and chatters and the dilapidated farmsounds of outer Ghost Town begin to thin, sink, and let themselves go, replaced by the satisfied analog hum made by all happy things.

Colt is cooking chili on top of the woodfire stove, stirring, with our one rag tossed over his shoulder the way James Dean would shoulder a leather jacket. Precisely careless. He is wearing only his Levi's. The fact that he has no belt on reveals that he had not been only minutes ago. As I watch him cook, he is smiling, something cowboys do not do often.

While he stirs, he turns his head to look at me, still lying on the rustled bed.

"Hey beautiful," he says, "You feelin' alright?"

I am feeling alright, better than, and I tell him so.

I look down at myself, shocked to see the thin naked body of a human woman reclining on the bed. *This is me.* I seem to know already. I admire the subtle curves of my physique, trace the dip of my waist with my own fingers. I feel the perk of my breasts down to the empty fork of my legs and then back again. I am warm and soft and wet and more myself now than walnut and blue steel could ever be. *It's perfect,* I think.

I sigh more audibly than I would like, but Colt just chuckles and looks over with his clear blue eyes. They outline me and then color me in, making me a more complete picture than I was before.

"Everything okay, Winnie?"

He sets down the chili, smirking because he knows that, yes, everything is okay, it could not be better.

I nod and then follow him with my eyes as he walks towards the bed slowly. The sun fades gently and the night gets darker until the only people on the planet are the two of us in this cabin right now.

Morning After

I wake up feeling freshly manufactured.

Last night's dream was a drug. I had never dreamed, or imagined dreaming, before Colt brought me home to his cabin. Even after that, it took years before I started mind-wandering during the night. Lately, though, the dreams have been getting more frequent, more lucid.

I used to just dream simple things, like Colt and I's peaceful porch-nights, or him and I lying in the grass on a sunny day, the glint of my steel making my cowboy hard. On bad nights, I would dream about my barrel bending sideways, my bullets missing the squirrel that Colt was aiming me at.

But it had been a few months now that I was dreaming of different things altogether. Impossible things, like growing slender human limbs and walking through the forest of my own accord. Like romantic nights in the cabin where Colt and I can be together in new, more perfect ways. It has become commonplace for me to wander into an imaginary world where Colt can hold me like he would a woman. Where we could lay on his tiny bed together, and he'd whisper *Winnie* in my ear, a real, actual ear, and for the first time I would hear the vibrations of his voice like everyone else does.

This morning, it is especially difficult to stay grounded. Last night's dream may have been the realest, most impossible yet, and the fading sunlight and chili smell cling to my senses.

Next to me, Colt is breathing sleep. It must be early still.

I remember the dream-feel of warm hands on skin and sigh. Audibly.

I startle myself so bad I almost jump. I've never sighed before, not really, not out loud. I notice that for the first time I can feel the softness of the bed sheets, and the imprint of warmth that a body leaves in its wake. To my surprise, I push myself up onto elbows, actual flesh and bone elbows.

I look down at everything attached to me. Just like the dream, I am made of human meat. I have arms and legs, small breasts and a slim, tender belly. Just like the dream, my body seems to have become completely human.

Except for one thing. One little thing.

Between my legs, where in the dream I felt the lips of a vagina with my own fingers, I have a section of gun barrel melded to the damp skin of my crotch. It's not large, thank god, but the little piece of blue steel protrudes as a reminder of what I used to be.

I clench my eyes shut and pinch myself. The pain of the pinch on top of my little steel phallus tells me that this is not a dream, no, this is simply tomorrow. Only instead of having the body of a Winchester Model 1873 rifle, I now have the skin and bones of a human woman.

I love it. Joy surges through my body like a gunshot. I swing my legs off of the bed and stand up, careful not to wake up my cowboy just yet.

Colt doesn't have a mirror in his cabin, so I look at my new body in the reflection of the windowglass. It's beautiful! I feel like I am trying on a floral dress cut perfectly to fit for the first time. A feeling of home-ness that I had never realized was missing. I do a couple spins, take in every freckle and curve. I smile at my reflection, and it smiles back with a full row of ivory teeth. I spin back to face the reflection. Looking down, I wrap my hand around the barrel-tip between my legs. The only thing different from how I dreamed it. The midnight metal is pliable enough that with some effort, I am able to tuck it back far enough to hide it from view. It's uncomfortable, but more than worth it. In the glass reflection, I see a gorgeous woman. She looks reinvigorated, young but not adolescent. Her skin is smooth and it glows. She puts her hands on her slender hips, smiles, and then waves at me. I wave back. I eep out a sound like a small animal, unsure exactly how to verbally express excitement.

I twirl in the glass reflection one last time, thinking, *Hello, Winnie, it's nice to finally meet you.*

Then I turn to face my cowboy, still asleep on the bed despite the sun beginning to stream in.

I muffle a barely-controllable giggle fit and make my way over to him.

You're the only girl I'll ever want, the only one I'll ever need. His voice echoes in my head.

I can't wait to see what he thinks.

THE SPOOK

It used to be Colt would take me to a little dive in Ghost Town. It is a dirty brick building with a sign nearly falling off the roof. The sign is cheap white plastic and it just reads *Henry's*, or at least it did before it aged fifteen extra years. It doesn't really matter what it says though, because everyone in and around Ghost Town calls it the Spook. The Spook is the only bar left in town. All the old bartenders and town drunks died the night the town aged.

Inside, the Spook is dark and a handful of old men always drink silent beers at the vinyl-and-wood bar. Colt sits close enough to hear the old men whisper, but far enough away that they won't drag him into conversation. He pats me and leans me against the bar down by his feet and order a Coors from the tap.

This is a Friday night habit, has been for a while.

This Friday it has been almost a year since Colt bought me. Like all the others, he takes me to the Spook, sits on his stool, and leans me lovingly against the bar. The bartender, Wrinkles we call him, a man whose face looks too old for the rest of him, walks up to where we are sitting.

"Whatcha need, cowboy?"

"Coors."

"Uh-huh."

Wrinkles returns in a moment with a beer, and Colt nods his thanks.

I lean against the bar below, content to listen to Merle croon "Tonight the Bottle Let Me Down" and Colt slurp the head off his lager. Tonight, like most nights, Ghost Town is living up to its name. I watch Colt casually survey the clientele, glancing over both shoulders to see in panorama. Besides the old men guffawing and slapping the bar's red vinyl, it is just us and Wrinkles.

It stays like that for ten minutes, long enough for Colt to suck half his beer down.

Then the door to the Spook opens, the light from outside cutting a path to the far wall. Everyone turns to look, because in a town as small as Ghost Town, in a bar as empty as this, that's what you do. Just as the jukebox clicks over to Def Leppard, a woman walks in. With the bright light behind her, she looks like one of the silhouettes that adorn the mudflaps of every truck around. Other than myself, I don't know much of women, since the only places I had been in my lifetime were Colt's cabin, the gas station, and here, all places dominated by ballcaps and musk.

The door pocks shut behind the woman, who fades from a silhouette to a full rendering of perfection. Wearing short denim shorts and plaid, she materializes every Daisy Duke fantasy the men of the Spook have ever jacked off to. Even Colt, who I had never heard mention interest in the existence of women, can barely hold his saliva in.

Daisy Duke looks at all the open mouths and finds the one she wants tonight. Colt is young, burly, and attractive enough to capture her attention. She walks over to where we sit, intention clear in the click of her boots on the floor. I don't have to hear her speak to know I don't like her, but she does anyway.

"Hey, cowboy," she says. "What's your name?"

"C-colt," he stutters. His blue eyes are those of a teenager.

I feel pressure building inside me, and not the good kind that comes from Colt's fingers.

The woman sits down on the barstool next to Colt, and pulls my barrel towards her with a boot tip.

"I'm Mildred," the woman says. "This your rifle?"

Colt nods.

"Winnie," he says. "Winchester."

I am furious. I can't feel for myself, but I swear my steel is hot to the touch. *Stop talking to her. I am your only girl.*

"It's pretty," Mildred says.

It?!

She glances down at the bulge of Colt's jeans. "Got anything else long and hard you wanna show me?"

Colt doesn't answer immediately, mumbling empty syllables, so Mildred puts her hand a little too far up his thigh.

I can't take it anymore. Colt says I'm his only girl. His *only* one. As in nobody else, as in no fucking Mildred or Martha or Mary-Jane, as in just me. I feel like I could scream, like I could explode.

With Colt still tripping over his breath, Mildred leans in closer to him, tongue licking her cherry red lipstick.

"Well?" she asks, drawing the word out an extra beat.

Before Colt can say anything in response, I scream.

Everyone in the Spook duck-and-covers when they hear the gunshot, unsure of what just happened. Colt is covering his face with his forearms. He unfolds them, then stands mouth agape. After I scream I black with rage for a moment, but when I come to my senses, I see what I have done. Mildred's body is slumped over on her stool, neck hanging open like a fat, bloodthirsty leech. The ceiling above the body has been repainted dark red. Scattered in a wide fan behind her, all the way to the wall, are the tiny pieces of bone and meat that had been her smart-talking head a minute ago.

When the noise settles, Wrinkles starts yelling at Colt. He pulls a shotgun out from under the bar and waves it at us violently.

"GET. THE. FUCK. OUT OF MY BAR!"

Colt turns and looks at Wrinkles, staring right at him and pointing at the door Mildred had recently come through.

"NOW!"

Wrinkles reaches for the phone on the counter behind him. He dials three numbers and puts the receiver to his ear.

Colt seems foggy. I don't know if he is angry or just confused. How will he treat me after this? I've never killed anyone before, even accidentally. This is a new bridge to cross.

Colt shakes himself into a semblance of coherence, grabs me and runs out of the Spook.

We've never been there since.

Recoil

When I wake Colt up to show him the new, beautiful me, he loses it.

While he is still sleeping, I bend down and whisper breath into his ear. I want to say something like *good morning, handsome* or *wake up, sugar,* but I don't yet know how to carve words from my vocal cords. As soon as Colt feels my breath, his eyes shoot open and his pupils turn to big black tunnels. Instinctively, he pushes this new intruder away from the bed and reaches for where I would be lying if it was any morning before this. My untrained body can't keep balance, so I fall to the floor and pull my knees up to my chest.

Colt's fingers baffle around the empty space on his mattress for a minute, his sleepthick eyes clearing to take in the naked, huddled woman on his floor.

"What the *fuck?*" is all he says.

He sits up and looks through his sheets with wading arms for any sign of his beloved rifle. Finding nothing, he looks down at me. He seems to be trying to look through me, as if for evidence that I'm some sort of apparition or dream.

"Where's Winnie?" His inflection is a gun pointed at my head.

I smile at him and uncurl my legs, a full body arm-raise of innocence.

Please, don't shoot.

I try my best to open my legs seductively, letting my little rifle barrel flop into view. I try to tell him that this is me, look at me now, isn't this wonderful, but by the way Colt screws his face at me, I might have been bleating like a newborn calf. It occurs to me that everything that has ever been said between us was a chopped, screwed, and sugar-dipped interpretation my mind fed me. *Have you ever understood?* I want to ask. *Have you ever loved?* This whole time, maybe, our thoughts were only warning shots over an empty field aimed at nothing in particular. Bullets passing in the dark.

I make another noise, a quiet moan, and stroke my barrel with fingertips. Colt analyzes me breasts to barrel-tip, but he does not smile. His face remains blank but for the equations written across dense eyebrows.

"Where's Winnie?" he says again. This time, I hear the question in his voice, the vulnerability of admitting to knowing not, a lowering of the gun at my head.

He knows the answer, even if he doesn't believe it.

Colt puts his head in his hands as if he is going to cry, though of course he won't.

Cowboys can't cry.

I stand up, pad over to the bed on virgin feet. I sit down next to the cowboy. Next to the hulk of his torso, my new body is waifish. I sidle up to him and attempt to put my arms around his waist, but he pushes me away like a sick dog fending off a thermometer. His head remains in his hand for a minute before he slams his fist down on the mattress. He hits my thigh with the outburst, and I feel something new, a shot up my spine that reverberates in my skull. The skin on the top of my leg begins to marble black and blue spreading out to grey. I prod the new coloring and another shot rings in my brain.

Colt seems unaware that he hit me. He stands up and spins around, still naked. The sight of the man standing over me is bear-like. I begin to cry though I don't know what it is I am doing. I'm confused for a second, trying to gather up the tears with my hands and push them back into the holes of my irises. Colt takes a strong step forward then stops. He sees the bruising on my thigh and the rain on my face.

"Aw, fuck," he says, gesturing at me with an open-slap hand, "look what you've did."

I cry harder.

Colt looks at me like he looks at a deer he shot too young. Softness followed by a sharp edge.

"I mean," he says, his volume winding up for the pitch, "What am I supposed to do without a rifle? I need it to hunt, and, shit, for protection out here. I won't be able to eat! If I get attacked, that's fuckin' it! You can't just turn into a...you can't just *do* this like it's not gonna affect me! It's just...." He huffs. "Selfish."

"Say something!" he says after a moment. I can't. "Fuck this, I need a drink."

Colt pulls on his jeans quickly as if he was woken by a fire then throws on whatever t-shirt is closest. He grabs his boots and, without putting them on, slams out the door.

I listen to the cougarcry of Colt's old Ford come to life, and curse it for its will still being at his mercy. The two of them growl away.

My walnut-colored eyes are waterfalling, and it's only ten in the morning. Hours later, I'm still sitting on the bed of a cowboy who feels like a sudden stranger, my nascent skin wet with the hours of hurt draining out my eyes. In a fit, I yank at the barrel between my legs, hoping that I can just pull it out of me, separate the rifle from the woman. Then Colt could choose exactly what he wants. The only thing that happens is a painful stretching and a slight tearing at the base. Blood trickles down my bruised thigh and I let go.

I hear the phantom of the truck grumbling away and am reminded of a day it quit on him. Colt was out of beer and cigarettes, and he was going to take me into town to restock for the week. But when he turned the key to start the rusty heap, it just sneezed itself dead. After cussing open the hood of Old Faithful and digging around in her guts for a minute, he slammed her shut again. Without word, he spun on his heel and walked off toward town, leaving me alone in the cab of the truck.

I remember lying there til dark, unable to do anything but wonder where he had gone, afraid that maybe he had left us forever.

A few hours into the night, though, he had returned. Drunk as piss, but he was back. He patted the Ford's door then pulled me out of the open passenger side window.

"Come on, Winnie," he said, patting Old Faithful again, "we'll get her fixed up tomorrow."

I wipe my eyes and stand up from Colt's small bed. Once again, I approach my reflection and dare to marvel at this new skin I am wearing. I turn around, reveling in the feel of it like you would clean sheets.

How could you say no to this?

I twirl around on the balls of my feet and throw my arms out. I run outside. The big, blue mountains in the distance are washed with sunlight that pours down their slopes and collects in this little valley, making the grass seem even greener. On new legs, I race around the field in front of Colt's cabin, stopping to listen to what the trees have to tell me. Leaves and needles dancing, they shush my fears that I am abandoned. Colt will come around. He just needs time. I dance around more, and then fall back into the tall grass, letting it tickle my naked skin.

FIRST WORD

It is dark when Colt finally returns, Old Faithful scooting to a stop as he drunkenly smashes the clutch and brake with one boot. The engine dies, and he half-falls out of the driver's seat onto the ground. He gets up and shuts the door behind him.

I have been waiting for him on the porch of the cabin all day. *Like a good girl,* I think.

I spent the day learning a trick for him. A gift to surprise him with when he finally came home. The *Co* sound was easy, just shape the *O* with your lips and breathe out quickly, but the it took me hours to learn to tag the *lt* on the end.

When I hear him coming back, I say his name to myself a couple times to practice.

I see the glow of his truck lights and spring up, dancing around like one of the desperate squirrels Colt would aim me at while hunting. The truck stops and dies, and for a moment the shape of the man inside sits quiet and still.

"COLT!" I yell, breaking the silence. His only

response is to fling open Old Faithful's driver side door, abruptly illuminated by the triggered light of the cab.

Colt steps out of the truck, taking a second to catch his balance. He wobbles on his toes and then back to his boot-heels. He swims his arms to finds a rough center. Pretending he isn't too drunk to walk, he adjusts his hat then bumbles forward towards the door of the cabin. I want to rush him, but I wait until he gets closer to address him again.

"Colt!"

He does nothing.

I smile and squeal and extend my arms to help him walk. He stumbles ahead as if he were alone.

"Colt?" I ask.

I walk just inside and watch while the drunken cowboy falls on his cot like a mountain pine, limbs all splayed. The mattress screeches and exhales a cloud of dust as his body makes impact. Within seconds, he is snoring and the night is quiet besides.

I close the cabin door behind me, then walk over to the cot. With the little strength I have, I push Colt's snoring corpus far enough over to make room for me. I lie down in my usual spot, enjoying the perfume of my skin mixed with his. Soon I am asleep.

DENIAL

I awaken to the feeling of my body floating off the mattress. My eyes flutter open, and I yelp with confusion. Getting my bearings, I see that Colt has picked me up and flung my body over his shoulder. I laugh. This is how Colt used to hold me when I was a rifle, when he'd take me out to hunt. It's a funny joke once, but my stomach flips a bit at the recent memory of my riflehood. I push on Colt's head playfully to tell him that I caught on.

No response.

Colt continues to walk out of the cabin and towards the forest a half mile off. I try to tickle his sides and interrupt the punchline as my arms hang down his back.

"Colt?"

Nothing.

Colt just walks forward, ignoring all of my prods and moans and wriggling. This isn't funny anymore.

I get it, I used to be a rifle, ha ha, put me down.

I try to say this, but a series of empty syllables fall

out of my throat. Colt's only acknowledgment of me is a frustrated huff. *Fine.* I fall limp, rubber-spined, and hope that I'm put down soon.

After a mile or so of walking through the woods, Colt stops. His breathing, which had been becoming thicker from the exertion of carrying a rifle the size of an adult human, now thins to a whisper. I feel him softly sidestep closer to a large pine a few feet away, hugging to its trunk.

What the fuck? But I know.

A piece of a sound escapes my lips, and I am suddenly whipped off of Colt's shoulder and swung under his arm. A still of this moment might have captured a stoic cowboy awkwardly bowing a naked beauty at the end of a waltz, but a closer look says different. Muttering some ancient cowboy prayer, Colt aims my head at a small doe a hundred feet off. He holds my body as straight as possible, pulls me close for optimum accuracy.

You can't be serious.

Colt's face says otherwise. There is no joke in the clench of his jaw as he calculates down the soft curve of my spine, still a rifle sight in his eyes, and pantomimes shooting the deer with my body as his gun. The doe continues grazing on whatever forest shrub it was eating, completely unaware of the superhuman act of denial it was just attacked by.

Colt cusses his faulty gun and loosens his grip on me, rendering me free enough to wiggle out of his grasp and fall onto the damp pine needle floor. I jump to my feet, angry now. The sincerity of his ignorance is almost impossible to believe. I push Colt's bear-ish body with all my strength and shoot him a *what-the-*

fuck look. Colt stares at me or through me, continuing to be content dismissing the fact standing before him.

"Colt!" I say. "Colt? Wha?"

I gesture up and down my body, pinching the skin of my sides as if to say *Look at this, this is flesh, this is human.*

Colt looks at me with eyes that are bullet holes through his skull. Then he walks towards me and gathers me up, once again throwing my body over his shoulder like a mock rifle. I wrestle his burly arm as he begins walking back in the direction of his cabin, but I can't seem to free myself of his grip.

Please stop, please. Stop. I find myself wanting to be anywhere but where Colt is, a feeling that before now I never thought I could experience.

For the first time today, I scream.

Colt says nothing as he carries me back to the cabin.

BATH TIME

When he walks through the door, Colt drops me on the floor like a too-heavy bag of potatoes. I land on the same leg he bruised the morning before and yelp. Colt's only response is kicking a kitchen chair a few feet away from me to the ground. The wood-on-wood smack sounds like a baseball bat making hard contact, but the chair stays silent.

This is not the first time Colt has thrown me around. He does this every time we fail to kill something for dinner. When I was a rifle, it didn't matter if Colt chucked me in a corner anger-quick because I wouldn't feel it. Walnut and steel are meant to stay strong. But the flesh I am now is vulnerable. She bleeds and bruises and screams when she is hurt. She feels every drop of pain rained upon her. I pull myself off the wood panel floor then crowd my body into the closest corner of the cabin. I crouch, pull my legs into my body and notice newly blued skin. Colt is chugging around the small space. He is looking for something, opening then slamming drawers and pushing piles of everyday rubble off the counters. His cusses are saliva-soaked.

I begin crying, surprising myself when I do. As a rifle, I had born these meltdowns with the grace of a prisoner serving a deserved sentence. But now, it's as if my core has become just as soft as my body. *And, maybe, just as beautiful.* I begin to smile as my eyes flood over, realizing that this is the release I have needed all along. These emotions are my own. I am no one's projection, no one's object. No more motionless, mouthshut bearing of this cowboy's lashing. No more creature-killing or guard-dogging. Even though I performed them sufficiently, the duties of a weapon were never mine. Now, it occurs to me they can't be. Since my transformation, I am incapable of performing the tasks I've always loathed. I cannot be a rifle, not again, no matter how much Colt wants me to be, and not even if I were to wish it so. This cabin holds no place for me anymore. There is a rifle-shaped hole inside it, but I cannot fill it.

I never want to be a gun again.

I will make these legs walk, and I will make these lungs scream. I will cry and feel and cry and feel and then dry my own eyes with laughter.

I need to get out of here, I think.

Colt's banging around subsides. I look up from the corner and begin to stand. He has found whatever it was he was looking for. Back turned to me, he places it on his mattress. Then he turns my way and walks closer. His face is now clean of curses and upset eyes. He is even smiling, a smile like a skull-print bandana folded over and worn as a mask. He reaches out as he gets closer. I press my body into the wall.

"C'mon, Winnie. Time for your bath."

We both know what he means. I look past Colt at

the bed, and my fears are confirmed. On the sheets is a shoebox. There is white tape stuck to it and written on the tape in marker are the words *Winnie's Bath Toys*. It was a whimsical nickname, a joke that was funny when it was harmless but not anymore. I knew that inside that shoebox was the rod, patches, and solvent he used to use to clean my barrel when I was a rifle. Even though I am new to this body, it isn't hard to guess that those tools will now do me nothing but harm.

I push myself farther into the wooden wall. It seems my best chance at getting away is to outrun him, which I think I can maybe do. Colt is strong, but he isn't fast. I bolt to the left of him, the side facing the doorway, but I run into his burly arm and am stopped in my tracks.

Colt wraps his arm around my waist and picks me up. His expression is polished stone, as if he has become a statue of himself. If he truly intends to attempt to clean my new body, he has to be cruel or crazy or both. I feel like I could be sick as Colt carries me to the bed, sits down, and lays me across his lap, like I child he was preparing to spank. I try to wriggle off his lap and onto the floor, but he just presses a giant hand onto my back to hold me down. With his other hand, he opens the shoebox, threads a patch through end of the cleaning rod, and pours solvent into the cotton. He flips me onto my back and brandishes it like a cat toy in front of my face.

"You missed the deer today, but that's okay," he says. "I know you're a good rifle. We'll clean you up and make sure you're in tip-top shape. Get you clean as a fuckin' whistle. You'll be a good rifle again."

This is what Colt always said before, and he had been right. When I was a rifle, the burn in my barrel after a cleaning would baptize me of sin. The next day, I always seemed to shoot straighter, to be the rifle he wanted me to be. We'd bring home the catch, and Colt would tell me, *good girl, Winnie, you're the only girl I'll ever want, the only one I'll ever need.* But now I see it was never a girl he really wanted.

"Tomorrow you'll be a good rifle again," Colt echoes himself.

Holding me down with his elbow to keep both hands free, he pries my mouth open with one hand and shoves the poisoned rod down my throat with the other.

My screams are muffled by solvent-soaked cotton.

ESCAPE

At this point it seems like I've been running for hours. My legs are fresh at this, so there has been a fair amount of stumbling as well, like a bad horror movie, except that, as far as I can tell, Colt's not after me. Maybe he doesn't realize I'm gone yet, but probably he doesn't care. Whatever bond we had when I was a rifle turned to dust now.

I allow myself to stop and look back for a second. The only thing I see are the patches of vomit left in my wake. I can still feel the cleaning solvent burning inside me. I continue running.

Bath Time, cont'd

It is apropros, cruelly so, that Colt's favorite George Jones tune is "He Stopped Loving Her Today," the lead single off the 1980 album *I Am What I Am*. It's a song that, many times, Colt had beckoned out of the jukebox of the Spook with his pocket change, and a song that he would hum along to once he made it back to the bar stool with me leaning against the bar by his dangling boots.

This is also the song that Colt is humming as he shoves the cleaning rod, dipped in solvent, down my throat. I choke as he forces the tip of it further and further past where anything but food should go until I feel the tip of the rod rubbing the lining of my stomach. A cascade of unused juices explodes from my mouth. It coats Colt's hand and forearm and the mattress beneath with a sound like a truck through mud on a rainy day. With a disgusted look on his face, Colt pulls the rod out of me. I puke again as it leaves, feeling the vacancy it left fill itself in. A solvent-burn overstays its welcome.

"Oh, nuh-uh," he says.

Colt whips what vomit he can off of his arm and the cleaning rod by spanking me with it. The thin metal bites the skin of my ass. The spider-legs of a cruel idea crawl up Colt's face as I whimper in pain.

"Nah," I say, unable to fully form the word *no*.

My syllable doesn't stop him.

He flips me around and begins to shove the bile-covered cleaning rod into my rectum. I can feel it stretching me straight like a second spine as it makes its way through my intestines. A snail-trail of gun cleaner now burns through the length of my insides.

"Feelin clean yet?"

I nod and muffle an affirmative sound at him. He wriggles the rod around a few more times and then pulls it out of me so quickly I collapse. Then he rolls me onto my back so that I can see his eyes. They look bruised.

Colt chuckles. His eyes trace me down to my crotch.

"So you like that, huh?"

I feel his stiffness poking into my back. I force my head up to see that my barrel is sticking straight up like a proud traitor.

I didn't like it. I didn't like it at all.

As he contemplates my hard steel, his expression turns from humor to uncertainty. He looks at my member as if it was a tempestuous snake that could bite him. He inches a hand towards it, then pulls it quickly back to him as if reassessing his move.

In one move, Colt stands up and dumps my body off his lap. I land with the squelch of overworked organs. I don't move from where I land.

"We'll try again tomorrow," he says.

I lie on the ground until I have heard his clothes hit the floor. Until he has gingerly stepped over my body and creaked into bed, and until I hear the deep rhythm of his snoring float over me.

Then I run.

PUKE TRAIL

I'm standing in the middle of the road, watching the puddles of puke slowly soak into the gravel. I worry they will betray me, that Colt will track me down with them like a bleeding animal. I send them a wish not to give me up, but I know they have no choice in the matter. I hold my breath and try not to vomit any more.

I continue down the road. Up ahead, I can see the glow of the gas station at the edge of Ghost Town where Colt picked up beer and smokes. I continue towards it, admiring how peacefully unnerving it looks, illuminated in the dark like the mirage of a ghost. As I get closer, I can see how the white lights have aged to a viscous yellow. I walk up to the door. The place is closed of course, this late in a town like this, but I look inside. I see the dirty bootprints on the tiles in front of the register, the stacks of cigarettes on the shelves behind. It exudes warmth the way an old photo of a childhood home might. Some places stay beautiful even after horrible things happen. Or they become beautiful because of them.

I pull myself away and continue to walk down the road. No trucks pass me with their nightkilling headlights, which I am thankful for. I don't have the nerve to risk strangers right now. The burning in my intestines has abated some, but it reminds me to keep moving.

I do.

DOWNTOWN

It is still dark when I make it into Ghost Town maybe thirty minutes later, passing the Spook on the other side of the street like a kid afraid of a home that is told to house ghosts. I chase the memory of Mildred's exploded head from my own, a reinvigorated burning in my gut slamming the door behind it.

The lights here are nearly all dark, the gas station behind me being the brightest around. The houses and store fronts on either side of the street recline on their haunches like mountain lions waiting to pounce. I move through them quickly, afraid that maybe the people inside are no kinder than the cowboy. Better to risk it on my own.

I wander closer to the middle of town, where a handful of buildings three stories tall dominate the skyline. The downtown cluster rises up on each side of the street far enough to block out most of the moonlight. I keep to the shadows, watching for movement as I clutch my stomach. The town is dead. If there is anyone around, they are hiding as deliberately as I am.

I don't know where to go from here. Colt never took me downtown, so all the streets are equally unfamiliar. I stop next to a window in which a sign reads *CLOSING SALE*. I realize that I am tired, truly exhausted, and that my body has given what it can give in its poisoned state. My legs are beginning to crumple beneath me as if they were made of tin. My breathing slows and deepens and my heart downshifts to first. I continue down a road I don't know the name of. My skeleton crumples. I puke one last time before my vision turns off like a midcentury television, two curtains closing around you like the jaws of some behemothic shadow.

LAST STOP

I wake up to darkness. Against my skin I feel the rough felt of the inside of a car's trunk. A sudden shifting of the space I'm in and the rattlesnake whirring of six cylinders confirm that I am indeed in the back of someone's car. I feel around and finger every seam I find. I finally touch the cold metal of the trunk door's latch, but no amount of pulling will force it open. Must be locked.

"DOREEEEEN!"

I hear the voice calling from what I assume to be the front of the vehicle.

"GODAMMIT, DOREEEEEN!"

The words fly out the window and fade quickly into the street behind.

I continue to struggle against the latch. I kick at the door, but it barely budges from its closed position. It enters my head that all the racket I am making may be cause for a quick pit stop and a beating by my captor. Even though there is no acknowledgment of my existence from the cab of the car, the fear of retribution stills my movement and breath. I escaped one torture. Maybe if I'm lucky I can escape another.

My head slams the side of the trunk nearly hard enough to knock me out as the vehicle jerks to the right with a screech.

"DOREEEEEN!"

Thirty more seconds and then the Velcro tear of hard braking on a gravel lot. The car comes to a quick stop, and I'm thrown against the side of the trunk. A door opens and slams and boots crunch towards me.

"DOR!" The trunk opens and the volume of the voice cranks to eleven in my ears. "REEEEEN!"

I look up at my captor. A scruffy young man in a stained white t-shirt and a leather jacket looks down at me, long greasy hair nearly obscuring his eyes. They seem to look through me, as if I do not have a face to focus on. He growls with frustration as he bends into the trunk, picks me up, and hefts my puke-sick body over his shoulder.

I see where we are for the first time. It is evening, and the man holding me stands next to a beat-up mid-eighties Pontiac GTO. A white sticker on the rear window outlines a feminine form scarred by devil horns and a spike-tipped tail. I commiserate with the sticker-shape, knowing what it's like to be almost what you want to be.

The GTO's headlights shine onto the numbered door of a ramshackle motel. With one of its screws missing, the only way to tell that we've arrived at room number six is by the unpainted shadow of the number above the dangling nine. The two shapes combine to read sixty-nine, the digits artistically and accidentally arranged in a yin-yang spiral. The only other lights besides the rumbling vehicle's are the red-tinted moon and a neon sign in the shape of an octagon reading THE LAST STOP MOTEL.

The man carrying me slams the trunk of his car shut and then starts towards room six. He slings me off of his shoulder and into the crook of his arm. When he gets to the door I hear the impact of his boot on the wood and then the sound of screaming inside.

"DOREEEEEN!" the man says, seemingly for the millionth time.

He points my head through the door and charges in. Inside there is a dirty, small bed in which two women lie naked. One of them pulls the cream-white sheet over her breasts while the other pleads with her hands towards the man.

"Dick, no!" says the woman with pleading hands. "It's not what you think!"

"Like fuck it isn't," says the woman holding the sheets over her chest. Her drawl is soaked with nicotine. She raises it and addresses the man pointing me at their temporary love nest. "Doreen doesn't love you anymore! What's it gonna take for you to understand?"

The woman who is not Doreen begins to stand up but stops abruptly when Dick shakes me at them.

Can't anyone see that I'm not a rifle? I wonder.

"I'll shoot!" he yells. "Don't think I won't!"

With the last word, his voice cracks. I crane my head to look at him and realize he has started crying. He turns his gaze to Doreen, who hands still butterfly in front of her like sign language.

"How could you do this to me?" he asks, nose bubbling with snot. "And with her no less?"

He gestures at the woman who is not Doreen with my head.

Doreen finally drops her hands, and starts crying herself.

"She's right, Dick," she says. "I don't love you anymore. I'm not sure I ever did. I love her now. I love your mother."

The woman who is not Doreen looks at Dick smugly upon hearing this.

"Hear that, kiddo?" she says. "You lost."

Dick starts crying harder and louder and louder until he's screaming, flailing his free arm in the air like a toddler tantrum. He whips my head towards his mother and then pantomimes pulling a trigger located by my hip and the recoil of the two shots he thinks he has taken. When he sees that no bullets were fired, he relaxes his aim and looks me over with a mechanic's distaste for the broken object he's holding.

"What I get for picking up some random rifle," Dick says, wiping the tears off his face.

His mom stands up from the bed and starts to walk towards him.

"Sure fucked that up," she says to Dick, crossing her arms. "Now, why don't you go home and think about what you've done? I've got a job to finish."

Dick's mom chuckles and then bounces back on the bed at Doreen, who yelps and giggles excitedly. The two women begin to make out with loud, wet sucking sounds.

Dick watches for a moment and then slumps out of the room, shoulders hung, dragging me on the gravel back towards the GTO. I purr and struggle, but Dick does not acknowledge me. He lifts me once again into the trunk and slams it closed.

I feel the car start and whip around, speeding away from The Last Stop Motel.

FAILED SUICIDE

The GTO screeches to a stop. Boots crunching, then the trunk opens. This time I know what to expect. Dick looks down at me. He hadn't been yelling on the way back from the motel, but I see that his dead eyes are red and wet.

He pulls me out of the trunk and shoulders me. I look around and see that we are back in the downtown of Ghost Town. It's dark still, and quiet and empty. A breeze threads through the buildings and alleyways, whistling punctuation on the silence.

Dick sniffs up a nose full of snot. He walks into a nearby alley, leaving the GTO rumbling and awake in the middle of the street.

With me still on his shoulder, he looks at the clouded sky and shakes his fist, playing some bad script of a scorned male lover he must have seen in a movie.

"Why Doreen?!" he yells. "Why don't you love me?!"

He whips me off his shoulder. With his free hand he reaches into his pocket and pulls out a couple bullets and pops them into my mouth. I almost choke, but luckily I am able to keep them from going down my sore throat.

Dick sighs away his rage, and then holds me in an awkward hug. He lines up my head with his and then kisses me, if you could call it that. More that he tried to shove as much of my mouth as possible into his. I see what is happening and my stomach turns.

Dick pantomimes pulling a trigger by my hip. I spit the bullets into his mouth, playing along with his little charade. Dick lowers me, and then with tears in his eyes lets the bullets drop off his tongue.

"Fuck," he says, blowing air out his nose. His breath smells drunk in close proximity. "Can't even do that right."

He screams.

"FUCK this rifle!"

The wind shoots out of me as Dick throws me against the brick wall of the alleyway. I fall into a pile of trash and lose consciousness to the sound of boots stomping and an engine revving away.

My last thought before I sleep: *Not a fucking rifle.*

TRASH BAG LIMBO

I feel falling forever.

In my dream, if that's what this is, I'm drowning in a world of shiny black plastic bubbles. An anchorless place where there is no direction, breath, or time, only trash bags and trash bags and trash bags. Everything is floating, though I'm not sure you can call it that if there's nothing to be grounded upon. Smelly black bubble after smelly black bubble brush against me like a crowd of brutish and handsy strangers. I do my best to push myself towards anything, wading through plastic with frantic arms and legs, but it is unclear whether or not my efforts are fruitful. For hours, days it seems, there is just an unending, claustrophobic cyclorama of pure obsidian and my small, small body squirming through it but getting nowhere.

I don't know if I'm alive, dead, or something else entirely.

Finally, I begin to scream.

The sound is swallowed by the trash bags all around me. They soak my vibrations into their rotting slush, but it seems like they are moving away, slug-like, from me now.

I continue to scream and scream and scream, pushing the limits of my vocal chords for the first time since my they formed. The black bubbles sunder themselves, leaving an open void of empty darkness around me. I explore the space finally rid of stinking plastic, swimming myself aggressively at any nearby stragglers. The black bags continue to spread away like the particles of an atom separating. Continuing to exert my new freedom of movement, I see a small hole forming in the wall of trash bags. It expands as I swim and scream and flail and yell, letting a bullet-hole of light in. The light swirls around the void like a negative film video clip of food coloring dropped in a bowl of water.

I kick myself towards the hole with all of the strength I can gather. Slowly, slowly, my body floats at the source of light. It continues to grow from a pinprick to a flashlight beam then a spotlight. I have to nearly close my eyes, but I can feel warmth and I pull towards it with everything.

The blackness around me pales and pales until it becomes whiteness. I quit screaming, quit moving. I'm exhausted beyond breath. Then the whiteness around me melts and the outline of two dumpsters begins to crystallize, followed by asphalt and the brick walls of the buildings on either side of the alley. The scene clicks into full focus, revealing itself as an alleyway identical to the one I had passed out in before falling into that endless trash bag world. I realize I am lying in a small pile of plastic trash bags, although these are not black but bright and multicolored. I push myself frenetically up from the trash pile, not wanting to find myself in another existential loophole, even if it was more festively decorated.

Footsteps startle me.

"Quite a racket you were making."

I spin around, ready to do whatever I have to to get away.

REMY

A woman stands a few paces away from me, hands on her hips and smirking.

"Couldn't help but hear all that screaming. Everything okay, hun?"

The woman, like me, is not wearing any clothing except for a bright pink Stetson placed jauntily on her head. She is taller than me by nearly a foot and appears to be at least slightly older. Her body is toned and athletic, although naturally so, as if it was only a result of her everyday doings. I nearly gasp as I see that between her legs a double barrel protrudes proudly a good eight inches down her leg. She seems unaware that this is anything other than normal.

I stare at her barrel-tip for a socially unacceptable number of seconds, and she laughs. She half-tucks it between her legs, and I look away, down at my own barrel. The double barreled woman walks over to me, with the same hand she used to tuck herself extended.

"Hey," she says as she gets within shaking distance.

I reach my own hand out, too stunned by what is happening to properly shake hers back.

"I'm Remy," the woman says.

I stare at her face dumbly. She waves her hand in front of it.

"You got a name?"

"Winnie," I say. The name shocks me. Until now, the only word I could substantiate was the name of the cowboy, and even that took most of a day to learn. Saying my name here felt as effortless as if I had been speaking for years.

Remy steps a little closer and puts a hand on my shoulder. Looks into my eyes as if trying to read a story in them.

"Winnie's a nice name," she says, "but, if you don't mind my sayin' so, you don't look so great. Let's get you some water, and maybe have the doctor check you out."

I nod.

Remy guides me out of the alleyway and leads me down the street towards where the downtown dissipates. The layout of this place is the same as Ghost Town, but I get the feeling this is somewhere different. Instead of looking fifteen years dead, these buildings look freshly built, as if their ribbons had just been cut yesterday. The windows even seem clear of fingerprints and birdshit. Above the buildings, the sky is a crystal blue, and clouds wade through it contentedly.

As we make our way down the street, I also notice that there are many people walking around us. They all seem to be enjoying their strolls, wherever they are going. It doesn't take much looking around to notice that these are not like the people I have seen in Ghost

Town or the Spook. They look bright-eyed and clear-faced, unlike the downtrodden demeanors of Greg the gun man and the bartender of the Spook. Like Remy and I, none of the people here wear any clothing, aside from some accessories to personalize their nakedness. More noticeably, though, is that most of the people here have some part of a gun integrated into their bodies. Many have barrel-tips like Remy and I. Some have rifle butts for feet or the cylinders of a revolver for biceps. One person even has a pistol hammer sticking out of their skull like a metal mohawk.

Seeing all of these people around, people like me, going about their days cheerfully makes me smile. Remy sees me beaming and catches a grin herself, as she leads me towards where the buildings get smaller and more homey.

"Alright, hun," she says. "We're almost there."

WAITING ROOM

On the outside, the doctor's office looks like a small, pink house with white trim, almost like a life-size dollhouse. We walk up the porch stairs and in the front door. I expect to enter a room that is simple, quaint, and empty. I'm wrong. Inside is what looks like a waiting room. It is full of rifle people in various states of dismemberment, distress, and disarray. The few seemingly healthy ones wear pink aprons with pastel pink and blue bubbles printed on them. They rush around the room consoling the broken, bearing expressions that clash with their happily-colored attire. Many of the patients hold their stomachs, and the now-subtle pain in mine points to a similar reason.

Looking around, it seems that I must be lucky. I'm well enough to move about and speak, and it appears that many of these people are not. There is a man with triggers for fingers who is completely missing one of his legs, the remainder just a blood, steel, and splinter stump. He slumps into a purple plastic chair in a parody of consciousness. A kid with buckshot eyes vomits violently in the corner, the puddle they're creating ignored by the aprons as the least of their problems. The worst is a woman being carried into a bright yellow door on the opposite side of the waiting room by a few aprons. She's screaming, hands fighting to cover her crotch. As the aprons attempt to restrict her movement, I see why. Like me, this woman's reminder of her riflehood is a barrel-tip between her legs. Which is to say, it *was* her reminder. The only thing remaining is a bloody, metal-flecked ring where the base of it had connected to her. It's fresh enough that I can't help but wonder if the wound is self-inflicted.

Remy looks out over the crowd of patients, and her forehead creases chasms, the only sign she'll give of what she's feeling.

I'm not so strong. I lose it, completely.

I collapse into Remy, face soaking itself, and she holds me up from falling on the floor. Arms around my body, she leads me back out the front door into the picturesque front yard of the office. She sits us both down on the front steps.

"Why," is all I can say through tears.

"I don't know," she says. She sighs. "It's not always that bad. But it's not always that good, either. Believe it or not, you look like one of the lucky ones."

A handful of minutes pass, the only sound the muffled moaning of a hundred hurt gun-people. A breeze picks up, cooling the sun-warmed grass at our feet. My stomach still burns as it processes the poison I was fed, but after seeing the morbid state of the hospital waiting room, I can't help but think that I'll be just fine.

Any despair I have for my own pain is replaced by the pain of my kin. I look over at Remy, who adjusts her Stetson and continues to stare ahead. I get the feeling that I'm not the first person she's found dazed in an alleyway. Maybe that's what she does, finds us and gets us healing. Maybe she was the one in the alleyway at some point, and someone helped her. It occurs to me that these rifle people, that *we* must take care of our own if we are to survive. Cowboys won't protect us.

"Remy," I say. "I think I'll be okay."

"If the solvent was going to get you, it would've by now," she says. "The rest will heal with time."

She stands up from the steps, and I follow suit.

"Well then," she says, "let's get you some food."

I don't yet feel hungry after that scene, but I know food will do me well. It will help push the poison out, give me strength to heal.

Remy walks out of the front yard and turns left, heading further away from downtown. I run up behind her, then keep pace, hoping that one day my steps are as confident as hers.

UNICORN

We walk for long enough that I begin to wonder if Remy lives outside of town. The prospect of another cabin in the woods gives me chills, but I decide to trust her, at least for now. I recognize the houses we pass as lively doppelgangers to those I had seen the night of my escape in Ghost Town. Instead of greyscale and mold, these homes are decorated with bright colors from every end of the spectrum. Chartreuse, cyan, lavender, and rose. They are clean, new-looking, and well-kept. If homes could look happy, these were ecstatic.

We reach the building that in Ghost Town would have been the Spook. Curious to see what it looks like here, I crane my neck as we get closer. The small building appears to still be a bar, but like the other buildings it hardly looks old or decrepit. Where the Spook has ashy brick walls, this place looks like it is made of Legos. Each shiny brick is a different color, giving it a multi-chromatic glow in the sunlight. Shades of mint and mauve and melon melt into the air around the building. Plastered above the door are crystalline letters that spell *UNICORN*.

I want to keep looking at the wondrous bar, but Remy turns towards it and makes her way for the entrance. A closed sign floats in the glass of the door. Remy takes off her Stetson, reaches inside, and pulls out a mother-of-pearl key. She slips the key into the door and gives it a familiar turn. It opens. We walk inside, and as Remy passes the threshold, she reaches behind the door and flips a small hanging sign to show a side that reads *OPEN*.

LOVELY BUBBLE GUM TOWN

As I tear through two baskets of sweet potato fries, it occurs to me that I have never actually eaten anything. The pain of the poison and the lack of awareness around my new needs had never made it evident that, yes, eating was something I should do. I nearly lick the grease out of the basket the fries taste so good. I swear to never go hungry again.

Remy stands on the inner side of the bar I sit at, elbows resting on top. She chuckles at me and pantomimes checking a watch.

"Sometimes I forget how hungry you newbies are." She looks into the blank air beside my head. "It's been a long time since I transformed."

I stop licking salt and sit back, eyes still locked on the void left by the sweet potato fries.

"Where am I?" I ask, a question so obvious I had forgone asking it til now.

"By the sign out front you know you're in the Unicorn, which is my bar," Remy nods towards the door we had come in, "but I assume what you mean is, What is this town?"

I nod my affirmation and she continues.

"We call it Lovely Bubble Gum Town. The people that live here are mainly gun-people, like you and me, many of whom were spurned by their owners after their transformations. When we are guns, we are easily controlled by our handlers. They can hold us still and fire us when they want to. We make them feel safe, because with us they have the power to protect their persons and property, or to kill how they see fit. As I'm sure you know, many of us live up to these expectations with pride like well-broken dogs. But beneath that, many of us long for something more." Remy clears her throat and adjusts her hat, then continues. "And, for those like us, that longing can bear fruit. We are given new purpose through new flesh, though not without a reminder of our former selves. No one knows why some of us transform and some continue to serve. All we know is that those that owned us are often frightened by the power we are given with our new bodies. Power to move of our own will. To speak words instead of shoot bullets. Feeling naked without a weapon they can control, our handlers lash out at us at our most vulnerable, when we have just changed and are learning how to be human in our new skins."

Remy pauses. I swallow salt-taste. The story she tells is familiar, but I did not realize it did not solely belong to me.

"So how did we get here, to Lovely Bubble Gum Town?"

Remy shrugs. "Maybe there was a first, but all we know is that we all find a tunnel from Ghost Town, the same way you did. Sometimes it's in an alleyway, sometimes the hollow of a tree. Almost always, we are transported when we are hurt and near our end. I've seen many hurt like you, and many hurt worse. It never gets easier to see."

Remy smacks the bartop with a naked slap and smiles.

"But! Lovely Bubble Gum Town is a happy, bright place. You are safe here. You are surrounded by people who love and understand you, not people who will hurt you."

I nod and smile. What Remy is saying is evident based on what I've seen. Even though we arrive in the place in a state of distress, we are healed by standing together, by holding each other up.

I push the empty plastic basket towards Remy and bat my eyelashes at her. She takes the hint, laughs, and heads towards the kitchen to retrieve more fries.

"You want a drink?" Remy asks, pausing to wink over her shoulder.

COWBOY WITHOUT A GUN

Colt is crying, something cowboys rarely do. The last few days without Winnie have been some of the loneliest of his life. A cowboy without a gun is not much of anything. Left empty-handed, he can't help but feel like a shadow of what he thought he was without his rifle.

He remembers back (how many years now?) to days when he could still fit his favorite pair of firetruck pajamas. He wishes he had them now.

But lately Colt has spent more hours than not posted up at the bar of the Spook. Henry the bartender was starting to get annoyed, saying that a cowboy blubbering into a Coors drives away customers, but they both know that no one would come anyway, that Colt is not much of a cowboy anyway, whatever that means.

This town's closer to dead than ever.

At least he still has Old Faithful, Colt thinks, but she can't replace his beloved rifle. She only dims the pain.

At one point, Colt goes back to Greg's Gr8 Guns. He is drunker than Waylon Jennings on the fourth of July and thinks that maybe a new rifle will cheer him up. A younger, prettier rifle. A rifle that won't leave him alone like *she* did. It's only early afternoon, and the store is about close due to the lack of paying customers.

Behind the counter, Greg, old man become ancient, is trying to fit a small caliber bullet into his gums where a tooth used to be. He startles when the bells on the glass door jingle and swallows his homemade denture with a loud gulp. Looking though his glasses, he cleans them on his shirt then looks through them again. It's the young cowboy, now a good ten years older than when Greg had seen him last. The cowboy looks worse for wear. His white t-shirt is stained yellow-brownish from the armpits down. He sports a three-day beard littered with dried up chili crumbs. His eyes are wet and red and look like they could both be made of glass.

"Can I help ya, son?"

The cowboy stumbles forward a few steps, then stops. He makes a choking sound and stares at something behind Greg. Greg turns to see what the cowboy is looking at. Up on the wall, there is an empty space and a tag that reads WINCHESTER MODEL 1873 - $500 SALE. It had been a while since Greg had sold that rifle, and he couldn't remember who had bought it. But since there wasn't much in the way of business these days, he hadn't bothered to replace the empty shelf with another gun.

"You doin' alright?" Greg asks the cowboy.

Colt continues to stare at the space that he had first seen his Winnie, sitting there fresh and pretty as a dew-covered daisy. The Coors sloshes around in his stomach, and he vomits pure pilsner onto the floor of Greg's shop. Emptied and invigorated, he begins growling three words to himself over and over.

"Shit, son," Greg says. "All over the floor? And what the shit are you yammerin' on?"

Greg cups and hand over his ear to try and hear what the cowboy is saying. The chant gets faster and louder and more intense, and finally even Greg's old ears can catch what the cowboy is saying, each syllable a pistolshot.

"Gitter back. Gitter back. Gitter back."

VISION

"What's this?" I ask Remy, grabbing the glowing bubble-shaped glass she had just placed in front of me.

"It's horn juice," she says, smiling. "Our specialty down here at the Unicorn. Take a sip."

The horn juice is a marble of green and pink that swirls in endless shapes as if a spirit were stirring it. The rim of the glass is covered in blue crystals that seem to be giving off steam without ever melting. I look down into the glass a second but take a sip when Remy chuckles at my hesitance.

"It won't hurt," she says. "Quite the opposite."

As I take a drink, my nose fills with the blue steam ghosting off the rim. It smells like rain, and I feel it immediately soak into the folds of my brain. Though I don't know what many things taste like, I guess that the pink and green liquid tastes like something that comes from the forest. A pine-sweet scent mixes with the rain in my nostrils, convalescing into what mountain fog early in the summer would taste like if it could.

As soon as I swallow, I am met with a vision of a girl. She is knee-deep in a lavender pool in a copse of long-pine evergreens. She is young, and she steps out of the pool gingerly dressed in nothing but leaves and instead of labia she has the barrel of a gun between her legs. I realize that this girl is me, younger than I remember ever being but full of joy. She laughs and looks through vision-walls right at me. She says nothing but with her eyes, which tell me *you have not become anything you were not already.*

Then she turns and begins to run off, joined by two other children. They hold hands and melt off into the trees, following the sound of music.

"I told you it wouldn't hurt."

The words bring me back to the bar stool where I sit, horn juice in front of me.

"I saw..." I begin.

Remy shushes me with a finger.

"We all see what we need to," she says.

"Is it always like that?" I ask.

"The first drink is. It's like an initiation. I give horn juice to all the newbies when they make it to Lovely Bubble Gum Town."

"But what is it?"

Remy smiles big enough to show her teeth.

"Secret recipe," she says.

HORN JUICE HIGH

I wake up in a mint green bed that feels like it's made of a pile of beach balls. I try to roll myself out of it but find my limbs struggling against currents of bloated mattress and air. I wonder how I slept on it last night without falling off.

How we *slept,* I remind myself.

I didn't stick with one glass of horn juice. Remy keeps them coming, to no complaint from me. The more I drink, the more I am filled with a heady contentedness towards everything and everyone around me. The many bright colors in the Unicorn weave together to create new, brighter colors.

As the day goes on, I am greeted by a river of regulars to the bar, each one enthusiastic to tell me what their favorite part of Lovely Bubble Gum Town is. One of the regulars, Phosphene, sits down with me for most of the night. They have one grey eye and one socket filled by a dark lead ball. A newcomer to the social graces of

Lovely Bubble Gum Town, I ask them, Is their marker, their reminder of riflehood, like Remy had said?

"No," they say, seeing some memory in a glass of horn juice, "I am lucky in one way and unlucky in another. When I transformed, I became exactly how you see me now, complete with two working eyes. But one was taken from me during my escape from my owner. I was not his only weapon, see?"

I nod. They were shot by their own kin. I apologize for asking and vow to tread lighter with my questions next time.

At closing time, the only ones left are Remy and I.

I am nearly swimming in the thickness of the atmosphere around me, yet each thing I focus on becomes more clear than it had been before. Remy becomes one of these details, leaning over the bar across from me. For the first time, I notice the small breasts that protrude from her body with large pink nipples topping them like the garnish on a dessert. She looks me in the eye, and I look back. The clarity of her irises had eluded me before, but now I see each fractal of the crushed crystal they are made from. She winks one quickly closed and smiles. Her lips are overripe and painted blue.

"Looks like everyone's gone now," she says. "Need a place to stay?"

The answer is obvious, but I nod yes and let her guide me to the back of the Unicorn.

GUNLOVE

Remy devours me, and everything within. She turns me backwards inside out and shows me shapes I didn't know existed. This is my first time, doing whatever this is. I realize I'm not quite sure yet but I love it.

She weaves me, threads fingers and tongue and rifle barrel through me like sugary silk string. She pulls me like pottery and architects a town in my hollows. I become a balloon animal for her, pressure building in every inch of me.

A spine-crackle splits the horn juice high, which melts away. I begin to feel like my skin is a neon sign turned full blast, and each time Remy touches me, she ups my amperage. She strokes me onto my knees and palms and gently shoves fingers then barrel inside me, pistoning slowly first then fast. My barrel stiffens as she fills me up, and each thrust births more static in my spine. Everything builds and crumbles and then rebuilds on top of it, and then with a bang we fire beautiful blanks, her into me and me onto the fabric of her bed, which I now realize looks like home.

She pulls herself out of me, and I pull my body into hers. The night turns from warm silence to sleep with the faint whisper of skin on sheets.

NEWCOMER'S DAY

The next morning we are downtown, and the streets are full of color. Every shape and size of rifle-person has shown up to line the sidewalks. Remy woke me up with breakfast and a small glass of horn juice, and once I'd finished drug me out the door without giving hint of our destination.

"What's going on here?" I ask her, as she leads me by the hand to the end of a line of young rifle-people.

"Today is Newcomer's Day!" she says, smile shadowed by the brim of her pink cowboy hat. When she sees the question on my face, she continues. "Once a year, we hold a parade for all of the new citizens of Lovely Bubble Gum Town. We celebrate ourselves as a family of rifle-people, and celebrate that many of us have escaped bad people and places and made a new home here."

She gestures at the shiny buildings and multiplicity of people around us. I realize that I may not have known what *home* really meant until now.

PARADE

Remy and I take our place in the parade procession. All around us, gun-people have decorated themselves in colorful paint and fabric. Cadres of musicians play melodies on instruments of all kinds, found and built by hand. The music trails through the air like a million smiling, psychedelic snakes. The parade-goers stand on either side of the street cheering us on as we begin to move, to march ahead. Remy nudges me forward as the procession starts.

As we walk along, the spectators on the sidewalks throw multicolored wads of paper at us. A pink wad falls in front of me and I pick it up as I pass. When I uncrumple the paper, I see that it is cut into the shape of a pistol with a sort of speech bubble emerging from the tip of the barrel. Inside the bubble is written *The Only Ammunition You Need Is Love. Welcome! –Sara.* I pick up another paper and uncrumple it. It reads *Every Part of You is Perfect. –Devon.* My eyes get wet as I read paper after paper, all with messages of love and welcome from the citizens of Lovely Bubble Gum Town. I join the cheering and music, reveling in the sound of all of our voices joyous together.

The parade travels a couple of blocks through downtown when some of the marchers ahead stop. I hear the reason. Over the sounds of celebration, I begin to hear a mechanic growling sound that takes me back to Colt's cabin outside of Ghost Town. The rumbling gets louder. The chorus of cheering and speaker music ceases as everyone looks around for the source of the noise. It sounds clunky and guttural, as if the gears of a giant wristwatch were turned to overdrive. By the confused expressions around me and Remy's uncharacteristic silence, I can tell that this is not a part of the normal Newcomer's Day festivities.

I bump into the rifle-person in front of me as the parade comes to a complete stop.

The grunting enginesound swells swiftly, and then I hear a thwack followed by screaming, cracking, and the organic squelch of flesh on asphalt. I watch in horror as Old Faithful emerges from the cross street a few yards in front of me, piloted by a stoic cowboy. Without expression, Colt drives the old Ford through the crowd directly in front of me, crushing over the bodies like he was the entertainment at a monster truck rally. Blood sprays across the chrome grill and windshield of Old Faithful, which screeches to a stop once Colt sees me standing in the parade.

The bodies of at least twenty lie lifeless on the street. They surround the truck like boatwake made of bone and blood, splayed outward. Many of the bodies are dismembered, their pieces creating a pile of unclaimed limbs and torsos and rifle parts. Their blood begins to gather in a lake around the wheels of Old Faithful, a lake whose surface is angrily broken by the leather heels of an old pair of western boots.

As he steps out of the cab of the truck, Colt surveys the carnage around him like he is a contractor giving a new home final inspection. When he has verified that everything looks in order, Colt adjusts his Stetson and lets out something like a sigh of relief.

Nobody moves, afraid of the murderous stranger that has just smashed their kin into wet gravel. Colt turns his gaze to me. He smiles.

"Well, there you are!" he says. "I was wondering where you'd gotten to!"

He holds out his arms like a person beckoning a hug from a child. Standing behind me, Remy puts her hand on my shoulder. My clenched jaw slacks slightly. I hadn't told her about Colt yet, but her grasp is knowing enough. She seems to have seen this before.

Remy is the first to answer, stepping in front of me protectively.

"And you are?" she says.

"Name's Colt," Colt says. He offers no other explanation. Neither one of them moves from their place. "Howdy."

Remy stares bullets at the cowboy.

"You're not welcome here," she says. Her voice is boiling.

Colt scratches the back of his neck. He looks around for a moment, eyeing all of the gun-people that stare at him with fear or hate or both. His brow hardens.

"To be honest, I can't say I'd want to be a part of this gun show," Colt says. "I'm just here to get my rifle back. Take it home. Then I'll leave. Promise." His gaze drops to the ground around him. "And sorry about the...others."

Remy takes a step forward, pushing me back a few feet.

"There are no rifles here," she says. "Only people. And you had better get going before we get too unhappy."

Colt takes a step towards us. As he moves away from Old Faithful, I notice that his wrinkles seem to soften.

"Look, I just want what's mine," he says, sharpening his tone. His voice seems to get higher. "Then I'll be off like a shot. No harm done."

Remy looks at the bodies that swarm Colt's blood-wet boots.

"I beg to differ," she says.

Colt takes another step forward and loses a few inches in height. If he notices, he plays it off as if he doesn't.

"It's an expression," he says, voice shrilling.

"It's a lie," Remy retorts. She stands her ground.

The cowboy advances on her with mad-steer steps. The farther he gets from his truck, the shorter he shrinks. It occurs to me that, in Lovely Bubble Gum Town, there has been no aging. Things here are not nearer death or dying like they are in Ghost Town. Here, Old Faithful must be Colt's only link to Ghost Town, and the further he steps into Lovely Bubble Gum Town, the more the aging is reversed. As he advances, his beard begins to fall out, and his clothing bags on his diminishing body. He wobbles in his boots as his feet start to swim in them.

He continues forward slowly like he's stalking a deer.

By the time he gets to Remy, he appears to be a

young teenage version of himself. His head barely reaches Remy's breasts, and he looks up to meet her gaze.

"Give me my rifle," the child Colt says. His voice is prepubescent and squeaks on the word *rifle.*

A few in the crowd of parade-goers laugh.

"I said there are no rifles here," Remy says.

"Give. Me. My. *Rifle!*" child Colt says. He crosses his arms and makes a pouting expression. The anger that was so terrifying when Colt was a full grown man becomes laughably annoying now that he has been turned back into a child.

Remy grabs child Colt by the hair and drags him towards an alleyway that I recognize as the one I appeared in when I first arrived at Lovely Bubble Gum Town. The child Colt flails his arms and tries to bite at Remy's legs like a rabid dog, but the woman is too strong for him. His body falls give-up limp and he starts crying quietly. Remy disappears into the alley with the blubbering kid and exits a few seconds later empty handed.

She walks towards me and grabs my hand.

"Won't have to worry about him anymore," she says.

I wonder if Colt is headed through the trash-bag filled limbo that I fell into on my way here. I spend a moment worrying for his safety, but soon forget when Remy squeezes my hand.

She points at Old Faithful. A crowd of parade goers have cleared away the hurt and dying, and through tears carry them off towards the hospital. A group of others breaks away and follows them, a squad of gunpeople ready to provide emotional support for their broken comrades. A final group approaches the old truck that used to belong to Colt. In their hands, they hold colorful paints, streamers, and an assortment of decorative fabrics and materials.

"Wait!" I say.

I cut myself off when the group continues towards Old Faithful without any sign of aging.

"We aren't citizens of Ghost Town," Remy says. "Neither are you. None of us can be affected by the curse of it."

She pulls me close for a moment, and then leads me towards the old Ford. The crowd begins painting over the peeling rust orange, draping it with beautiful fabrics, and decorating it with sequins and glitter. In a few minutes, what used to be a dirty old truck becomes a parade float to rival any other. A group of rifle-people jump in the back and begin singing. The musicians in the parade that had quieted begin playing again. Remy opens the door of Old Faithful and gestures at the redecorated cab. I climb into the truck, entering it for the first time since my transformation. Remy gets in behind me and shuts the door. She rumbles the float to life and, after checking to make sure everyone is safely out of the way, she turns it towards the parade's destination point ahead.

As we drive on, the music plays and the people cheer. The street is a joyous flood of color. I hear a jangling by my feet and look down to see a Coors can bouncing around in the wheel well. I reach down and pick it up. On the golden metal there are tobacco stain fingerprints, the only reminder left of the cowboy that used to own me.

With skin and bone fingers, I crush the can in my hand and then toss it as far as I can out the passenger side window.

THE NEW LIFE

The shudder of the old brakes coming to a stop makes Winnie vibrate with excitement. This new person in a cowboy hat picks her up and carries her out of Old Faithful with a newlywed's care. She floats through the air on someone else's wings, content to let the breeze blow away at the silence.

The sky is bright today, and clouds marble the otherwise clear blue-grey atmosphere that stretches out above them.

Winnie's insides sputter nervously as she is carried inside, and into bed. Sheets feel soft and evening-cool on her body. She lies there for a few minutes until she just melts away, thoughts of what this fresh life will hold for her chasing each other into, out, and around her mind like so many summer-free children.

THE FIRST DAY

Colt sits down on the bed next to his new rifle, petting the polished surface of the varnished woodgrain. He misses his grandparents, despite their endless, puritanical bickering.

The farm died, and the town died, nearly enough, and what small hand he was dealt in the world has been taken from him. He is young, but not too young to know that now, now and forever, it is just him against whatever gets in his way. After a few days of sleeping in the graveyard silence of Ghost Town's empty outskirts, he found this cabin. It's small, but it's something. Whoever used to own it is probably dead and gone and won't be coming back for it. And anyway, he found it, and he's a grown up now, and look at these hands, suddenly big, suddenly beaten, suddenly able to grab whatever he wants from life and just take it. *I'm a cowboy, a fucking cowboy,* he tells himself, glancing over the reflection of him in his grandpa's old Stetson in the cabin window. *And a cowboy doesn't need anyone, a cowboy just needs one thing, that's it.*

Colt draws finger guns at his reflection and makes a Dirty Harry face. His new, older body is actually intimidating, actually believable. He walks over to the bed and picks up the Winchester he has just purchased using money he had found in the furniture depths of his grandparents' farmhouse. *She's a beauty*, he thinks. He aims the rifle at the window reflection and admires the cowboy he sees holding him at gunpoint.

After a minute, he grab a Coors from the half-empty eighteen-rack he had purchased yesterday and carries it with his new gun out to the porch and sits down. He cracks it open and sips, still unused to the metallic, warm taste of it. Not sure he likes that, the taste, but he does like how it makes him die inside, just like his grandparents died on the outside. He likes how it makes him forget that inside this body, a twelve-year-old boy is crying over the corpses he found, over the death of the farm, over parents he doesn't know the name of who aren't there and who can't tell him it will be alright even if it isn't. The world is a scary place to find yourself in when you're not even thirteen.

Colt shakes off the thought, pulls out a dart, and lights it.

He may not have parents, or grandparents, or much of a home, but he does have one thing, and that's the one thing every self-respecting cowboy needs.

Colt has a gun.

Katy is a queer trans woman living in Seattle. Queer is a Katy Seattle woman living in trans. Woman is a living Seattle Katy trans in queer. She likes cats.

F4
Larissa Glasser

A cruise ship on the back of a sleeping kaiju. A transgender bartender trying to come terms with who she is. A rift in dimensions known as The Sway. A cruel captain. A storm of turmoil, insanity and magic is coming together and taking the ship deep into the unknown. What will Carol the bartender learn in this maddening non-place that changes bodies and minds alike into bizarre terrors? What is the sleeping monster who holds up the ship trying to tell her? What do Carol's fractured sense of self and a community of internet trolls have to do with the sudden pull of The Sway?

Polymer
Caleb Wilson

You've seen monster hunts before. You've watched as a guy with throwing axes and ninja stars ascends stairs to fight a big furry werewolf with tentacles or a floating head of indeterminate origin. You've seen hunters. But you've never seen Polymer. Polymer's got style, Polymer's got sex appeal, Polymer's got panache. And you, lucky reader, get to join us right behind the glass in Sickleburg Castle where the battle of the century is about to commence. Who is the man behind the music, the monsters, the guts, the gore and the glory? Get ready for an event like no other.

Winnie
Katy Michelle Quinn

Winnie and Colt forever. Winnie is Colt's one and only, Colt is Winnie's true love. Winnie is Colt's rifle. There is nothing Winnie wants more than to please Colt and since a rifle is everything the young cowboy's ever wanted, she certainly does that. But one day Winnie finds that she is not a rifle but in fact a woman. Can Winnie keep the sparks between them ignited, even if she isn't the gun of his dreams. What happens if she can't?

Eviscerator
Farah Rose Smith

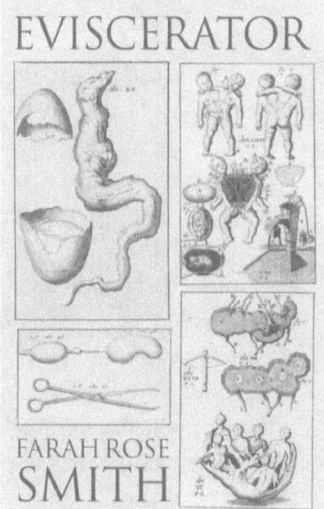

Vex Valis—doctor. Vex Valis—rocker. Vex Valis—iconoclast. You would think Vex Valis has it all but what Vex has is a secret that rots away at her from her very core. Vex is infected with Gut Ghouls and will do anything to be rid of them, even if it means consorting with subterranean worms or blending science and the occult in dangerous and unsavory ways. You may envy Vex's jet setting Dark Wave scientist lifestyle but you won't when you see the trials incurred when she catches the attention of a being that rends people and worlds alike, the scrutiny of...The Eviscerator

Fell Beauties
Leigham Shardlow

In the last outpost of ugliness in the world, beautiful people are falling from the sky. When Fat Janet is kicked out of the buffet where she has holed up for food and safety, she is forced to confront not only the reality of perfect falling bodies but the attentions of an overzealous plastic surgeon and his followers. She teams up with a mystery man in hopes of getting out of this alive but soon finds that confronting the problem head on is the only option. Can imperfection survive this beautiful disaster?

Crime of the Scene
Shawn Koch

A detective investigating a crime scene finds that nested inside this crime scene is another, and inside that another. Demons, physical deformity, body switching and endless trials await him as he begins to face his own transgressions. Reality grows distant as he soon comes to realize that he has stumbled not only upon the scene of many crimes but of all crimes. He might just have what it takes to get to the bottom of these but only if he gets to the bottom of himself.